A BETTER PEARL

Once upon a time, there lived two girls called Pearl and Ellen.

Pearl was beautiful; she had long curly hair.

Pearl loved to sing.

Whenever Pearl was singing, everyone stopped to listen to her.

She had a very beautiful voice.

Pearl would sing when she was bathing, playing, or walking to school.

Pearl would always sing, and as she kept on singing, her voice got better.

On the other hand, Ellen was beautiful, kind, and compassionate.

She lived in the little town where Pearl lived.

She loved music, and although she didn't have a sweet voice like Pearl, she didn't mind.

She lived close to Pearl, so each time she heard pearl singing, she would stay by her window and listen to her.

Pearl and Ellen attended the same school and were in the same class.

Ellen would volunteer each time the school had an event; however, Pearl was too proud.

She would sit back as if she was a queen and watch others do the work.

Each time they pleaded with her to join them to sing for the event.

She would refuse they would have to kneel and plead with her, and they would also buy her.

All she wanted before she sang at the school event.

Ellen was more than happy to help; however, she didn't have a voice as good as Pearl's.

Pearl was the best singer in the school.

She knew this just like everyone else; she also liked the attention they gave her.

The gifts she received each time an event was to take place at school.

One day, Pearl's teacher called her, saying, "Pearl dear, you're a gorgeous girl, you're smart, and you have a beautiful voice.

However, I have noticed something not so beautiful.

You seem to have a little bit of pride in your voice and beauty.

Being confident about your talent is okay, but you should not let it get in the way of how you see others.

It would help if you were willing to use your beautiful voice to make everyone happy.

Not make them plead all the time to help, and not make them feel they are less important because they can't sing like you.

Remember that everyone is special.

"However, Pearl wouldn't listen.

She felt she was better than everyone because she could sing so well.

One day, the school and the community wanted to have a big event.

The children from the school were to sing at the event.

As usual, Pearl was to be the lead singer.

For days, they tried to convince Pearl to sing.

"Pearl, please sing with us at the big event,' they said to her.

"Why should I sing with you all?

Your voices are bad,' Pearl said to them in an unpolite tone.

"You'll be the lead singer; we'll just be in the background," they told her, and she smiled.

"You all aren't worthy to be my backup,' she said to them.

The children were unhappy with how she spoke to them, but because they needed her, they didn't walk away.

"What's in it for me? Pearl asked.

"We'll give you all you want," they told her. "Fine, I'll sing," Pearl said.

They thanked her and told her the place and time for rehearsal.

Ellen couldn't sing, but she went to rehearsals to hear them sing.

When it was time for rehearsal to begin.

Pearl was nowhere to be found; they waited for over an hour.

But Pearl didn't show up, and they couldn't start rehearsal without her.

The kids were sad and discouraged.

"Hold on, everyone, I'll run home and call Pearl.

Maybe she forgot," Ellen said.

Ellen ran all the way home to call Pearl when she got to Pearl's house.

Ellen knocked, and Pearl's mom opened the door and asked her to come in.

Ellen saw Pearl watching TV.

"Pearl, here you are everyone has been waiting for you at the rehearsal ground," Ellen said.

"Shhhh, I'm busy; go tell them to wait for me; I'm coming," Pearl said.

Ellen ran back to the rehearsal, "she said she'll join us soon.

Why not we start," Ellen told them, they insisted on waiting for Pearl.

But after Ellen encouraged them, they rehearsed.

Unfortunately, when the rehearsal ended, Pearl didn't show up.

However, the kids were happy with themselves.

Ellen was there to encourage and cheer them.

"Ellen, you should join us," one of the kids said.

"I can't sing," Ellen said. "You can just sing from your heart," they told her.

Ellen joined them to sing, she realized that her voice wasn't as good as theirs, but it wasn't so bad.

By the third rehearsal, Pearl hadn't shown up.

The kids went to her house to know what was wrong.

"Hello Pearl, we have had three rehearsals, but we haven't seen you in any of them," one of the kids said.

"Do you think I'll waste my time rehearsing with you all?

I don't need to rehearse with you; I'm good; you all need rehearsals."

Pearl said rudely.

The kids were unhappy.

They went away looking sad.

"Don't be sad," Ellen told them.

"I wish we could learn a song that she doesn't know.

When the big day comes, she wouldn't be able to lead the song.

Then she'll know that rehearsals are important," Henry, one of the singers, said.

All the other kids liked the idea, and together they prepared a new song.

They were still worried that they didn't have a lead singer.

Moreover, it was two days before the big event: there was one rehearsal left.

So, Ellen went to Pearl's house to convince her to come for the final rehearsal.

Which was held the next day.

"Pearl, we need you, come for the rehearsal tomorrow.

Please come; the other singers need you," Ellen said.

"You can't tell me what to do, Ellen, I'm the best singer, I decide what to do," Pearl said.

Ellen wasn't happy when she went to bed.

She couldn't sleep and was worried that the song might not come out well if Pearl kept acting that way.

Ellen fell asleep and dreamt that she had met a fairy.

The fairy told her that she would reward her with a better voice because of her selfless act.

When Ellen woke up, she forgot all about the dream.

When it was time for the final rehearsal, the kids sat down and wouldn't sing.

Ellen tried to convince them to sing, but they were discouraged because Pearl didn't show up.

"We can do this without Pearl: believe in yourself," Ellen told them over again.

They wouldn't listen to her. "Fine, I'll rehearse alone then," she said and went to the front.

Finally, Ellen began to sing, her voice came out so beautifully, and everyone was amazed.

"Wow, is that Ellen singing?" One said.

"I never knew she was this good," another kid said.

"She sounds better than Pearl," Henry announced

"It's true, I agree," they said.

"Ellen, please be the lead singer," they said to her when she stopped singing.

"I can't; Pearl will show up tomorrow, I'm sure, and she'll lead the song," Ellen said.

"Pearl doesn't know the song; you do, and besides, your voice is better than Pearl; please sing," they told Ellen.

"I can't," Ellen wasn't sure about herself.

She feared that her voice might go bad when she faced the crowd.

"A few minutes ago, you told us to believe in ourselves, belief in yourself, Ellen," they told her.

Finally, Ellen agreed to lead the song, the rehearsal was awesome, and the kids went home happy and ready for the new day.

They also decided on a change of costume.

They agreed to wear white against the blue they had agreed on before. The next morning, the event started, Pearl decided to go late.

So, the kids would be worried and grateful when she showed up.

She wore a blue dress and black sandals.

The kids sat at their spot in their white clothes.

They had smiles and couldn't wait to sing; they didn't even notice that Pearl was running late.

When it was almost time to sing, Pearl came.

When she saw that the others were putting on white and she had a different color on.

She was angry, "I'm not singing with you all anymore," Pearl said so they could plead with her as usual.

"No problem," Henry said, and Pearl was surprised that no one begged her.

"Fine, I'll sing," she said. "You don't know the song," one of the kids said.

"Thanks, not possible," Pearl said. The kids were called to sing, and Pearl ran out first and took the place of the lead singer.

Ellen didn't try to make a scene.

Instead, she stood with her backup.

When Pearl began to sing, and no one joined her.

She cried and ran off the stage, Ellen took the microphone and began to sing, and everyone joined her.

When they were done singing, everyone clapped and cheered the kids; they sang beautifully.

Pearl came later to apologize to them.

She promised that she wouldn't be proud because of what she had and that she would be a better Pearl.

Pearl volunteered first at the next school event, and she didn't miss any rehearsal.

THE END

www.ingramcontent.com/pod-product-compliance
Lightning Source LLC
Chambersburg PA
CBHW070734160726
48003CB00006BA/2498